4-11-23

To my Joan ~
~ who is already
an infinite possibility
much love now &
forever ~
Grandma

maybe

Written by Kobi Yamada • Illustrated by Gabriella Barouch

Have you ever wondered why you are here?

You are the only you there ever
has been or ever will be.

You have so much to offer.

Maybe you will invent something
that no one has ever seen before?

Maybe you will build things
that reach high into the sky?

Your life is yours.

Try as many things as you can try.
See as much as you can see.

Wherever you go, take your hopes,
pack your dreams, and never forget—
it is on journeys that discoveries are made.

Maybe you will help others
to see the beauty in each day?

Or maybe you will lift cheering
crowds onto their feet?

Do everything with love. Follow your
heart and see where it leads you.

PL XII

Maybe you are here to shine
a light into places that have
been dark for far too long?

Maybe you will speak up
for those who can't speak
for themselves?

Maybe you are here to help
in ways that only you can?

There will be struggles, there will be fears,
and it won't always be easy.

At times it will feel really hard.
And you might make a mess of things.

You may fall down.

You may fail.

But you will also get back up, and you
will rise a little stronger and a little taller.

Because there really is more inside you
than you know. And this world needs
your gifts, your talents, your big ideas.

And maybe you are just getting started.

What if you are only scratching the surface
of what you can do and who you can be?

What if you have talents
you haven't discovered yet?

There is something powerful,
even magical, about you.

You already have everything
it takes to do big things.

Maybe you have no idea just how good you really can be? And maybe you don't know how much you matter?

But maybe, just maybe, the world has been waiting centuries for someone exactly like you.

One thing is for sure, you are here.
And because you are here…

...anything is possible.

Dear Shale & Ever,
The quality of your life will mirror the
quality of the questions you ask yourself.
Love,
Dad

For my family,
Thank you for being my safety net
and allowing me to pursue creativity
with an open heart.
G.B.

COMPENDIUM®
live inspired

Written by: Kobi Yamada
Illustrated by: Gabriella Barouch
Edited by: Ruth Austin
Designed by: Jill Labieniec

Library of Congress Control Number: 2019900773 | ISBN: 978-1-946873-75-0

14th printing. Printed in China with soy inks on FSC®-Mix certified paper. A012207014

*Create
meaningful
moments
with gifts
that inspire.*

CONNECT WITH US
live-inspired.com | sayhello@compendiuminc.com

@compendiumliveinspired
#compendiumliveinspired